He is black from the tip of his nose
to the tip of his tail.

Ever since she was a kitten,
White Cat has been entirely white.

She has two white ears,
one white tummy and
four white paws.

She is white from the tip
of her nose to the tippiest-tip
of her tail.

Black Cat only goes out in the day.

He likes to watch
the swallows soar.

White Cat only goes out at night.

There's no better time
to gaze at the twinkly stars.

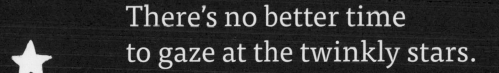

Black Cat has never seen the night.
Not even once. So he asks his friend Blackbird,
"What can you see in the night sky, Blackbird?"

"I don't know!" Blackbird replies.
"At night I'm asleep in my nest.
Why don't you wait until it's dark
and see what you can see?"

And **White Cat** has never seen the day.
Never ever. So she asks her friend Snowy Owl,
"What can you see in the bright sky, Snowy?"

"Don't ask me!" Snowy Owl replies.
"I'm fast asleep in the daytime.
Why don't you wait until it's light
and see what you can see?"

So that is what **Black Cat** does.
With a flick of his tail,
he sets off towards the night.

"Bye-bye, **Black Cat!**"
chirps Blackbird.

And **White Cat?**
With a twitch of her whiskers,
she sets off towards the day.

"Good luck, **White Cat!**"
hoots Snowy Owl.

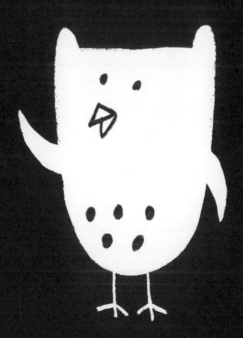

And that's how **Black Cat** and **White Cat**

came to meet.

"I'm going to find out what night is like," says **Black Cat**.

"Do you want to join me?"

"Oh! I'm going to see what day is like,"
says **White Cat**.

"Do you want
to join me?"

So...

White Cat takes **Black Cat**
to discover the night.

"Follow me!" she says.

Then **Black Cat** takes **White Cat**
to discover the day.

"I'll lead the way!" he says.

The night is full of wonder.

"*Purr purrrr*, look at those glittery, fluttery fireflies!"

And the day is full of surprise.

"*Miaow*, look at those busy, buzzy bumblebees!"

Black Cat shows **White Cat**
the most beautiful things of the day –
daisies, doves and butterflies ...

and **White Cat** finds **Black Cat** the most tasty treats of the night – snakes, bats and mice.

Day and night,

night and day ...

Black Cat and White Cat

are inseparable.

So inseparable, in fact, that they have

one, two, three, four, five, SIX ...

KITTENS!

AND CAN YOU GUESS
WHAT COLOUR THEY ARE?

ORANGE!